ANN AND SEAMUS

Ann and Seamus

KEVIN MAJOR

ART BY
David Blackwood

A GROUNDWOOD BOOK
DOUGLAS & MCINTYRE
TORONTO VANCOUVER BERKELEY

Groundwood Books / Douglas & McIntyre
720 Bathurst Street, Suite 500, Toronto, Ontario M5S 2R4

Distributed in the USA by Publishers Group West
1700 Fourth Street, Berkeley, CA 94710

We acknowledge for their financial support of our publishing program the
Canada Council for the Arts, the Government of Canada through the
Book Publishing Industry Development Program (BPIDP), the Ontario
Arts Council and the Government of Ontario through the Ontario Media
Development Corporation's Ontario Book Initiative.

The author acknowledges the support of the
Canada Council for the Arts.

Canada Council
for the Arts

Conseil des Arts
du Canada

ONTARIO ARTS COUNCIL
CONSEIL DES ARTS DE L'ONTARIO

National Library of Canada Cataloging in Publication
Major, Kevin
Ann and Seamus / by Kevin Major; art by David Blackwood.
ISBN 0-88899-561-x
1. Harvey, Ann 1811-1860–Juvenile fiction. 2. Despatch (Ship)–Juvenile
fiction. 3. Shipwrecks–Newfoundland and Labrador–Juvenile fiction.
I. Blackwood, David II. Title.
PS8576.A523A74 2003   JC813'.54   C2003-903265-5
PZ7

Design by Michael Solomon
Printed and bound in China

For the families who fished cod
off the shores of
Newfoundland and Labrador

I
Ann

ISLE AUX MORTS.
Who would ever want it said
they dwell in a place with such a name?
Who would not rather be born
to Rose Blanche, or Harbour Grace
or even Iles de la Madeleine?

Isle aux Morts — Island of the Dead.
The name in either language
is frightful to anyone
in heaven or on earth.

Yet upon the great sprawls of shoreline rock
is built our house.
We are the sole family
in this corner of our Newfoundland.

Here there are no trees
nor soil deep enough for a vegetable to take root.
Yet in the fall the scrub that fills the crevices
turns a scarlet red —
red so pure it makes your heart swell
with the beauty at God's hand.

A FEW MILES OFF OUR SHORE
the sea smashes against the jagged rocks
whipping, churning
into the devil's froth.
Sunkers these rocks are called.
Bad Neighbors.

In the fog they vanish.
Too many hapless ships
have ventured near
only to be cut abroad
and their
men
women
and children
washed lifeless upon the rocks.

FROM THE SOILS OF ENGLAND
our ancestors
transplanted themselves
to barren rock.

island to island

No government men followed
to build lighthouses
or church men
to bring the word of God.

England to its new found land

island to island

IT WAS THE YEAR 1811
that my lungs first felt salt air,
that I first laid eyes on salt water.

Father held me high
in his thick fisherman's hands.
He threw open the door
and bellowed
There it is, Ann, me young maid.
The sea.
Our lot in life.

I never cried
and never once
in all my young years
did I do anything
but take his words for true.

I am his first born.
I am his fisherman's maid
born to the ways of the sea.
Another five years would pass
before he had a son who lived.

My mother has been giving birth
as long as I can remember.
Time and again I am the one
to hold her hand and pray
for her pain to pass.
When I was a child
I prayed with my eyes shut tight
asking God to be quick
and make another little wrinkled one
find a way into our world.

When I grew older
I opened my eyes
and helped tug the baby out,
clear his nostrils of their slime,
help him get his first breath
of salt air.

Now there's eight of us all told.
No easy mission for any mother
let alone in a place without neighbors.

Hers is a weary world
and she too strong a mother to complain.
Besides the brood of us to feed
there's clothes to make and mend and wash,
a house to clean.
She is forever bending, scrubbing,
forever nursing someone back to health.
All that and working at the cod besides.

Is this the world my future holds for me?

Cod
is all the reason in the world
to settle in this cove.

Cod
fills our boat,
thick and lusty fish
some days in swarms as dense as fog.

Cod
to gut and split abroad
and wash and salt and spread
outdoors upon the rocks
to stack and store and spread again.

This, the reason we are on this earth —
to turn cod into dried salt cod
for the tables of the world?

My brother Tom is twelve
and as slick with a knife
as anyone who ever cleaned a cod.
When he steps aside
his job done
he clears his throat and spits upon the rocks.

I catch the eye of my father,
both of us smiling at his eldest son
thinking himself a man.

On bright and civil summer days
when the cod is spread and gleaming white with
    salt,
I sit on the shore
and think of the hundreds who will eat this fish
in lands far distant from our own.
I think of who might sit on their shores
in wonder about the place
from where their meal has come.

Idler, Tom calls, and spits upon the rocks.
Dreamer, I call back, and pitch a rock into the
    water.

I dream of books,
of reading and writing.

What Father knows is fish.
For books he has no mind or heart.
Mother the same.
What learning's here is fish.

But the fish merchant's sons have their learning
or how would they grow
to be merchants like their father?
Their daughters the same.
They have their books.

In St. John's schoolhouses hold hundreds.
In Boston even more,
the Yankee trader said it's true.

But we are so few and distant
no teacher will come live among us.

THE MERCHANT MAN
in Fortune Bay
keeps his home in England.

There his children go to school
and learn the ways of numbers,
the ways they fit in columns
and add to the family fortune.

Says he to us, in Isle aux Morts
you have no need to count money.
I will give you credit
and you will pay me back in fish
and if you show a profit
I will pay you then in goods.

The goods on my store shelves
are all you'll ever need, says he.
You have no need to count money.

For the merchant knows his numbers
and sets the price of fish.

My mother looks at me
and knows what questions dwell within my head
though she hardly has the time
to be giving me answers.
In her anxious eyes I see
someone who wishes more for her daughter
than she herself will ever know.

Mother, one day shall I read books?
Her answer is to scrub harder
at the clothes that crowd her wash tub.
She hands me the soap,
expecting me to do the same
and ask no more questions.

In the washing there is a rhythm
and in that rhythm a song —
a song only I can hear.
My mother Jane has too much
filling her days
to ever think
of singing.

My father George
will sing to his heart's content,
floating over the fishing grounds.

In the boat with him
I have heard his song filling the ocean
while he works his handline
in wait for its hooks to snag the cod.

But perhaps
a calm sea is made for singing —
the sun flickering on the water
and seagulls sailing high
above an ocean never ending

until it washes on some faraway shore.
Perhaps a calm sea is made for dreaming.

You're a dreamer, Ann Harvey
Tom says, grinning like the imp he is.
Keep your mind on the fish where it belongs.
You'll not see me craving silly books.
What good is reading
when all it will do is waste your time?

Tom, do you ever think of what's beyond that sea?

And Tom grins again.
Yes, he says, more sea and more fish.

Do you know that some your age have never seen
    the sea?

You're not in your right mind, Ann Harvey.
What do they do all day, answer me that.
What do they do if they can't catch fish?

FOR THE DEEPEST MONTHS OF WINTER
we leave this coast
and go for miles beyond
the farthest reaches of the bay
to a place in the woods
we call our winter house.

We leave behind fierce freezing winds,
ice glazing the shore
to settle among trees tall enough
their branches hold clouds of snow.

We do not settle there alone.
Other fishing families
turn inland
for the warmth of winter woods.

Among our neighbor's sons
is Charles, near my age.
A boy he is, his mind
muddling about in the body of a man.

When the families visit in the evenings
to talk around the fire
Charles hardly has two words to call his own.
His eyes keep wandering back to me.
I shift away
and hope, for his sake, that one day
his mind catches up with the rest of him.

THE OLD YANKEE TRADER
sails into Isle aux Morts
this spring with a new batch of stories.

Between his tea and rum he talks of gardens
where young ladies stroll with parasols
and gently touch their lips with lace handkerchiefs
and speak of gentlemen suitors and weddings.

He talks of dances
where young ladies in silks and satins
sweep down staircases
to dance the quadrille with young gentlemen.

Such a fine word, quadrille.
I run my hand over the trader's bolts of cloth,
over his silks and satins.
Who trades for such fine cloth?

No one along this shore, he says.
And as for the fish merchant in Fortune Bay,
his wife buys hers in England.

WE'LL HAVE A DANCE THEN, SAYS FATHER
if it's a dance ye wants.

He takes out his fiddle
and the Yankee trader a flute
while Mother clears the kitchen floor.

What will it be? says Father.
Round the Cape
or Buckley's Reel?

And in a wink the planks
are quaking with dancing feet.
Laughter fills the night
in our faraway inlet of the sea,
the only light the stars above
and the glow of the oil lamp
through our kitchen window below.

No time for discontent, Ann, me young maid.
There be lots worse off, me love,
lots worse off than we.

LOTS BETTER OFF, TOO,
if it be told.

God in heaven has his ways, I grant.

Praise be, utters my mother,
don't be questioning the Lord.
Have ye no religion, my girl?

Ye belongs to the Church of England, Ann.
That ye knows well enough.
We all belongs to the Church of England.

But I have never set foot in England
and never will as far as I can tell.

No odds, we still belongs
and we would read the Bible if we could.

Heed the commandments.
And thank the good Lord for the sense
to know what ye're about.

WHAT FORTUNE WE HAVE
is salvaged from the wrecks of ships.

Spars and pulleys, rope and rudders
surround our house.
Fine china cups painted in lacy swirls
lie in our kitchen cupboard.
Pieces of other lives now pieces of our own.

The Yankee trader claims the rope
for the yards of calico Mother will turn to dresses.

Will I forever dance in the misfortunes of others?

I SWIRL FREE IN MY DREAMS
a head full of notions
of other places
and other times

swirling now
whirling in the wind

and where will I come to rest
the question drifting about my waking hours
lurking through my nights

TODAY MY MIND SWIRLS WITH THE WIND.
Wild wind and fog and rain
drive us to refuge in our house.

Only Father ventures out
to secure his boat against the crashing waves.

He returns
stamping off his wetness,
throwing open the door,
his look as severe as the sea.

What is it, George?

Washed ashore, he says.
A keg no fisherman would own.
Stuffed with straw. Cargo under sail for weeks.

What do you make of it, Father?

A WRECK, NO MISTAKE, HE SAYS,
and our only course
to search for the hapless souls
who might survive these seas.

Ann, it'll not be easy.
The good Lord will be with us.
The wind and weather against.

Father pats the head of Hairyman
our dog, yelping his consent.

And what of me? says Tom.
I'm plenty man for the job.
I'll not be left behind.

Mother beholds her family,
her worry buried in silence,
buried with her fear of seas
as eager to swallow one of us
as give up any we might rescue.

AT DAYLIGHT
on this July Sunday
the year of Our Lord 1828,
with the light struggling through the fog,
we take to our skiff.

I scramble for the oars
as Father steadies her
thigh-deep in the pounding surf,
reckoning the waves
before pushing off and slipping aboard
all in one fitful start.

On the wharf dear Mother stands,
infant babe in her arms,
her cheerless young clinging to her skirts.

Their hands are raised
but ours are too busy to reply.
Mother's farewell nearly lost in the commotion.

The Lord be with you all!
Her words ride the wind
and we ride out the seas.
Pray! Father shouts back.
Pray we make it in time!

OUR SKIFF MEASURES
twelve feet stem to stern.
No great size to weather such swells
but many's the time she's done that and more.

Father and I man the oars.
Sometimes alone,
sometimes seated face-to-face,
his hands covering mine,
together fighting our way along the shore.

In the stern stands Tom,
hand clenched to the sculling oar,
eyes fixed for rocks.

Yes, and Hairyman,
as clever a dog as ever knew salt water,
his bowman's head into the wind
as if our work is to take him
to where he needs to be.

We are the crew.
Together we struggle
through the tumult of the sea,
the day breaking before us.

EVERY STROKE OF THE OARS
is a struggle for headway.
The coastline inches past.

And now
what meets our straining eyes
are scattered hunks of timber
flung savagely ashore,
piece heaped on battered piece.

There's no mistaking what we dreaded most.
The dog howls his alarm.
What sights await us still?

Row on and on we do,
fearful seafarers, fearful to the bone.
Past us sweep timbers freshly set adrift.

My God, shouts Father, she was no small vessel
whatever's left of her.

My God, shouts Tom, that's for sure and certain.

I am wordless,
straining, straining
to get past imagining the worst.

LOOK! MEN ASHORE!
Not a word but the startling truth.
Six of them desperate to be seen,
their cries lost
though not the wild waving of their arms.

We turn toward the land.
Steady, Father says, steady now.
We row toward the frantic, haggard lot
wading out to lead our boat to shore.

Thank the Lord for his mercy!
Their words the cries of men
freed from a wretched reef.
A reef, they shout,
that clutches two hundred more!

THE STORY THAT SURGES FROM THEM
is a grievous, horrific tale
even for this stretch of coast.

Vessel: the brig *Despatch*
Captain: William Lancaster
Port of registration: Workington, England
Port of embarkation: Londonderry, Ireland
Date: 29th day of May, 1828
Destination: Quebec City

These are the barest facts.
They tell us nothing of the misery and pain.
Woe are those who came into the hellish clutches
of Isle aux Morts.

Never was this home of ours better named.

II
Seamus

FROM COUNTY DONEGAL I COME.
Seamus Ryan is the name I carry
across the Atlantic, where I will make
for myself another life.

My Ireland is no place for
a man of eighteen years,
his family driven into the soil
by taxes and a damnable landlord.

Strong backs are needed in Quebec
and in Baltimore and New York I hear.
I might not tarry long
once my feet touch land.
I'll turn south to America,
as far away from the vile English
as I can get.

THIS BRIG OF OURS
is no fit shelter for so many souls.
We crowd a hold made for timber,
cargo that will fill the ship on its return.

We look the sorry sight
knowing not what awaits us
so far from the land of our birth.

But I for one care not.
I care to be free of the feuding
between us Catholics
and the bloody scoundrels
who plow us under with their laws.

I am one of the rebels,
one of Daniel O'Connell's boys
stoked in the fires of freedom!

And now I leave that too behind.
Gone I am, to make my way in a new world.

WEEKS SAILING A MISERABLE SEA
and no new world to be seen.

We sleep on bare boards,
the hold raw with the stench of vomit.

The young ones are the worst,
bawling for more at their mothers' breasts.
The old stay quiet
and let the misery wash over them.

I spend what time I can on deck
near the heat of the cooker.
We bide one day on potatoes,
the next on a stirabout of oatmeal
and not enough of either.

I am the eldest son sent ahead
because I am the strongest
and at the hedge school
we built behind their English backs
the priest taught me to read.

I will make way for the others.

Day after day
we wait.
The three weeks
promised
long since
past.

The water rations
miserly,
the food rations
insane.

The brig
is heedless
of time.
Will we ever
make land?

Day after barren day
we wait.

My thirst is for a better life.
It fills my every passing hour.
Yet I'll not give in to grumbling
for the sight of land.

The first mate, Henry, Captain's brother,
slips me a bag of hard biscuit
from his private store,
warning me to keep it hidden.

I can make do without it, Seamus.
You keep up your strength
for I can tell
you'll be making something of yourself
once we strike the shore.

That I will, by God,
and I'll find meself a girl at that.
Yes I will, by Saint Patrick
and all the saints in heaven.

Henry laughs.
I'm no Catholic, Seamus
but hold Saint Patrick to that, lad.

Look now, will you, Henry shouts.
You've not laid eyes on that sight before!
Swelling out of the sea
a monstrous slab of ice
filling half the sky.
Iceberg, Seamus.
Isn't it the devil's own size?

Suddenly the brig's astir.
Good God, where is it we've come?

A sign we're nearing Newfoundland, Captain
    shouts,
though we'll not be seeing much of it
for 'tis past its southern coast we're headed
and straight up the Gulf.

Our first taste of our new world is ice.

Ah, but Seamus, ice melts
and so will your troubles.

THE TALK OF LAND
brings a rush of souls
from the hold below.
Soon the deck is filled with eager eyes
peering past the ice
for their sight of the new found land.

And when it comes their spirits surge
as if the never-ending sea
had never drained their hopes.

Good Lord, she's a rugged isle
more rocky than our own.
Why would anyone
ever settle in such a place?

Cod, my man,
more than anyone can know.

And what we wouldn't give
for a taste of cod.
Over the side plummets a line and naked hook,
a rusted bit of chain for weight.
Up it comes,
as fine a cod
as ever swam the seas.
And like a mob possessed they are,
line and makeshift hooks and weights
flung for their chance at food.
Soon the cookers teem with fish
and around them cluster lusty gladdened souls
revived by the waters
off Newfoundland.

THE CHARMS OF THE SEA
do not last the hour.
Winds rise,
fog sets in
and soon the brig is
fighting its way to the Gulf
without any sight of land.

Our captain's steady at the wheel
though fear must shroud his face.
For nothing like this has he ever known.

Seamus, you're not afeared, are ye?
No, Henry, I'm not afeared.

Though my heart has ceased
its eager beat
at the thought of landfall in Quebec.
We'll ride out the storm
that now has turned
to a howling gale

and turned the *Despatch* into
a lurching vessel of seasickness.

HEAVE
heave, heave, you ungodly tempest
heave the brig
hurl her about the savage sea
clump of timber
set adrift

heave, heave, you monstrous swell
heave our refuge
cast it about the wretched brine
knot of shelter
set awry

Heave, heave, you blustering devil
heave, heave!

HAS THERE EVER BEEN SUCH FOG?
Such a thick and woeful veil
shrouding the coast?

I fear we cannot know
what we cannot see.

Seamus, Henry shouts above the wind,
the captain's a clever sailing hand
and we've plied these waters for a dozen years.

Still, such a grievous task!
A southeast gale howling relentlessly
and not the sight of land for days.

The chart his finger traces
is the work of Captain Cook,
and every rock and shoal it bears
are warning marks as sharp as razors

with that thick and wretched fog
burying every one.

Our captain's course is guesswork
forged by the brunt of winds.
He's abreast of the Cape Ray, he thinks.
Offshore twenty miles, he thinks.
Setting a course for the Gulf NW for N.

THE PASSENGERS SWARM BELOW
and mark their hours
with loud lament
and prayer.
Who's to know when this day will pass?
Who but God?

God will have his way.
As for me
I seize the rail
and let the demon of a storm
pound me like a heathen.

Seamus, get below deck!
As if I have not the sense
to be holding on for dear life.

Henry drags me
to what he takes for safer ground
just as the devil
slashes abroad the veil!

And shows himself —
a churlish, godless reef,
sharpened tongues of rock
slobbering in the surf.

GOOD GOD, WHAT WILL HOLD US BACK?
What will drag the brig astern?
What will save us from the doom!

The crew fills her foredeck
confounded at the sight of rock.
And I, mere landsman, a farmer's son,
I pitch and roll
my feet uprooted
my fate slung to the heavens

and waiting with arms widespread —
the godforsaken sea!

While from the hold
come the strains —
Rock of Ages
cleft for me.

I'll not hide myself
but stare it down,
be it more wicked
more ungodly cruel
than anything I've ever known.

The captain tears at the helm.
Shouts into the heedless wind
Hard down!

The brig has a mind of its own.
Hard down!
Smashes almighty waves across its bow
and rising up
headstrong in the swell

comes crashing down
onto that reef!
Timbers cleft abroad
on ageless rock!

TERROR SURGES IN.
The deck swarms
with petrified souls
herded by seawater
from down below.

Captain! Captain!
What's to become of us?
He has no answer.
Nothing he can say
we don't already know
from the grinding moan of timbers
against the cursed rocks.

Captain! Captain!
And before the words
have chance to wane
we see in his eyes
our only hope.
Quit the brig!
Fight body and soul
to get to a mainland
half a mile away.

The captain fires abroad his orders.
The studding-sail boom —
lower it to the rock!

That jagged strand of granite
washed senseless by the sea
is now a refuge.

HER SPIRIT MAULED,
the brig pitches to one side.
The lurch shrugs off the boom!
Another smack of fate
before the brute of a ship
settles down to die.

What now?
Out with the pinnace!
But before there's a gasp of hope
that boat is smashed against the brig,
its ribs spit into the waters.

The jolly boat then!
And from the stern
she's hoisted into the surf.
The dauntless captain
has set his mind on saving
the women and their piteous babes

with none the strength nor will
to face the frightful seas.

Captain! Captain!
Three hours he fights the surf,
he and two of his bravest crew
aboard the jolly boat,
clinging to the brig

until the fiercest of the waves
washes over them.

Captain! Captain!

He's the first to perish.

His brother swears
he'll not be following him
into that briny tomb.

SEAMUS, ARE YOU WITH ME!
Am I?
Will I man the long boat?

I'm no seaman,
no sailorman, no boatman.

You're hardier than most, lad.
Am I?
Am I not terrified to the bone?

If I don't take to that boat
what hope is there of rescue
from that god-forgotten rock?

Seamus, are you with me!

I am, Henry, I am.
And from where inside me
comes that brazen burst
I do not care.
No infernal sea will claim me
without a fight.

I stand ready for his orders.
Nearly trampled then
by the rush of bodies
mad to fill the long boat.
Nearly swamp the boat they do,
until Henry screams at them
and saves the wretched lot from drowning.

Atop the jib-boom I'm perched,
my courage naked,
the long boat lurching
in the seas below.

Henry edged this way before me
and dropped with oars into the boat.

Jump, ya gutless rat!
howl the vile hordes behind.

Jump, Seamus!
And jump I do,
just as the long boat
breaks free of the brig.

We toil at the oars,
clearing the rocks,
outlasting the swell
into wild open water.
Straining, straining,
braced to the seats,
pitching with the waves,
never giving up
until the shore
is in our grasp.

We spill from the boat
through the surf

onto the beach
past high tide
to the true
land-fast
barren
rock.

THERE WE COLLAPSE
wet, exhausted
forlorn creatures of the brine.

But alive we are,
free from the wreck
while those left behind
fight off death
at every wave and gust
and freakish wrench of timber.

The light fades
and with it mind for rescue.
We curl into sleep
tormented by wailing
we cannot hear,
though it must fill that loathsome reef.

Henry! I call through the wind.
Your brother was a brave man.

He was, Seamus,
and he died for his mistake.
How many more will follow him?

THE DAWN HAS NO ANSWERS.
The raging surf crushes
all hope of rescuing
the others from the reef.
Atop the highest rock
we scan their plight,
every man among us vexed with guilt.

We tramp the shore
and fret
and curse the wind.
No sign is there of man or beast.
No trace that any person
ever ventured near this coast.
No scent, no mark, no omen.

OUR TRAMP LEADS TO THE JOLLY BOAT
cast ashore, prodded by the waves,
a dead carcass lumped upon the beach.
Henry approaches it with tears.
His brother's doom.

Reverently, proudly
he leads us in turning it
upright.

The next day
the sea
offers its consent

and three of us set course
for the hallowed reef.

No LANDSMAN NOW AM I
lurching, heaving,
retching, ever mindful
of what the sea can do.

The sight that fills our eyes and ears
is of a sodden woeful band
clumped in mourning
expelling sharp confounded cries.

We give no thought to landing.
Amid the swell and razor rocks
faith lies in an end of rope
tied round a splintered scrap of wood
and flung into the surf.

It pitches and reels,
then lurches within our grasp.
A lifeline is secured.

And by fall of night
six of the strongest
drag themselves
between rock and jolly boat.
There to tell the tale
of some thirty more
lost in abandoning the brig —
overcome, washed away,
added to the captain's number.

SUNDAY DAWNS WITH A PRAYER.

O Lord in thy mercy
bless those departed this life
and those struggling
to hold to their fading breath.
Help us, O Lord, in our hour of need!

We huddle together about the beach
in the wake of Henry's words —
his tattered, famished, aimless crew
kept ashore by brutal seas.

A half dozen of the able, he says to us,
head in the bay along this shore.
Search for any sign of life,
anyone to aid us in our plight.

Now I am a leader of men,
be they a doleful lot
who think it a foolish quest,
who curse the barren vacant shore
and trudge on despondently.
Saved, they mutter, from a watery hell
to starve in hell on earth?

THEN, NOT A MILE ALONG THIS SHORE
despair is vanquished.
Hope seizes every soul!
A boat plying the open water!
No truer sight, dear Lord
has ever touched my eyes.

We hurl our arms into the air
and shout and yell
and praise Saint Patrick to the heavens!

The boat veers toward our shore.
The three aboard defy the sea
able as any oarsmen ever born.

Only when their gunnel is in reach
of our outstretched hands,
us waist-deep in the frigid water,
is it clear one's a young lad

and another a ruddy-faced girl
shouting at us to stay clear
lest we swamp their boat.

SAFELY ASHORE, SHE SMILES.
And I return it a thousand times
thankful for all eternity
to see another mortal's face.

Our grievous tale
hardens George Harvey's brow.
A plan takes hold, a scheme
sired from a lifetime on these seas.
His questions charge the air
while his boy passes round
glorious bread,
dried fish and water.

Two men hasten back with the news.
We others climb aboard the boat
and help row us all
to Henry waiting on the beach.

For a time the girl's hands cover mine.
Ann is my name, she says, her only words
though we stare face-to-face.

And Seamus mine.

III

Ann

His hands are frigid,
his eyes unsure,
though I'll not complain
for mine have little warmth to offer him.

Words break his salt-scarred lips.
The demon sea, he calls it.
No protest will pass from me
for who knows what else
this day will bring?

We're a miserable lot, he says.
Still, in his eyes
there is a vow
that one day a calm
will settle there.

This miserable lot has been cast
into our hands.
That demon sea has its curious ways.

ASHORE
they clench us in their weary arms,
wrap us in their wonder
at such a turn of fate as this,
such arousing hope!

Three boats, declares Henry Lancaster,
and a crew for each,
all skippered by a fellow
who knows this coast
better than anyone alive.
George, your word we'll follow to a man!

Father stares out to sea.
'Tis Ann at me oars and Tom in me stern
until I lay eyes on the poor souls
and what they're up against.

And with that he stares out to sea again.
Wait we do, and wait some more.

ALL THE WHILE SEAMUS LINGERS NEAR,
shamed by his ragged clothes
but sweetly brazen.

It is Ann, then, is it?
As if I have no choice but answer him.
Tell me about this Newfoundland.
The English rule this place?

Their fish merchants do, I tell him,
if the truth be told.

I look away
though not quick enough to miss
the way his mouth twists in proper scorn.

And what keeps you here besides the fish?
Your potato grounds?

Fish is all.

Fish is all, he says back to me.
And what do you do
when the fishing is poorly?

Make do, I tell him.
The same as when your potatoes rot.

His questions cease
but not the flurry of his words.

He talks of his family
and expects the same of me.
He talks of his country,
of his future,
and I have nothing to say.

He seems hardly to care,
content to hear his words
raw with salt
fall on someone
close at hand.
I think on his dreams,
asking him,
Seamus, what books can you read?

Any you might hand me, he says.
Could you not do the same?
I turn away, no liking for his idle pride.

SEAMUS, THERE IS WORK TO BE DONE.
Father has for him a task
for which his learning is no use.
Seamus, you in the jolly boat
and Henry in the long boat.
We'll lead in close
and fix ourselves
and I'll set in place a plan.
Steady, lads, says Father,
their fear in need of calming.

Tumult fills our day
and weariness our night.
Yet we are the fortunate ones.

To the rocks cling
a knotted clump of humans
fending off
the demons of the deep.
At the sight of our boats
their withered hopes
rise a pittance
and slouch again.

These seas are out to crush us all.
Fools we'd be
to draw closer.
Father sees but one hope.
And those peering from the reef
the same.

THAT HOPE FALLS
upon the shoulders of our dog.
At Father's coaxing
the pup flings himself into the surf
to fetch a floating scrap of wood
wound with an end of rope.

At the other end
hangs in desperation
every soul upon that reef.

Swim, doggio, swim!
His courage a beacon amongst the waves.
The sea would seem to swallow him
but up he comes with the wood
tight between his jaws!

Father grabs the rope
and piles the pup aboard,
our splendid sodden beast,
glorious champion of the hour.

OUR BOATS BATTLE THE WAVES,
the rope secured.
I work the oars, arms blind to pain
to brace the skiff, keep taut the line.
No let up, Ann, me young maid! Father calls
as kindly as that brutish storm allows.

Time and time again
dear battered souls
drag themselves
hand over hand
through the surf.
More times than not
in tow are loved ones
too weak to make it on their own.

Father leans over the bow, urges them on.
The good Lord is with you!
Father is their helper, their preacher,
their savior.

They reach his outstretched hands
hardly better than dead.

SIXTY SAVED BEFORE DARKNESS FALLS,
hauled aboard the boats,
landed ashore.
Sixty numb to all but hunger
and the smooth, dry, boundless rock.

Frailer than driftwood,
their bodies worn a haggard gray —
a battered broken lot
salvaged from the ledge of doom
to lie about the gates of death.

Come aboard with us, Seamus.
We'll need another back, says Father,
and another pair of hands.
Seamus draws every scrap of strength
as do I
and in the dark of night
we row without a word
the sickest home to our Isle aux Morts.

MOTHER, TOM CALLS, WE'RE BACK!
Cloaked in her nightgown and lantern light
she hastens from the house.

You'll not believe it, Mother.

What lies before her eyes
needs no words.
The creatures fill the night like phantoms.

She wraps them in blankets
and leads them to her kitchen.
They fall about the house
aching, hungry, delirious for sleep.

She soothes their grief with tea and bread
and gentle words.
You're safe now, me dears.
I'll nurse you back to health.

FOR MOTHER
there's us to warm with tea as well,
and watch
as we follow daylight out to sea

where pounding surf
drives us from the reef
worse than the day before.

By night more boatloads
we lead to Isle aux Morts
and clog our house
with fifty more
the sea had given up for dead.
Mother, her heart swollen
with their grief,
her weariness unspoken,
works on and on

far past the time when we again
follow daylight out to sea.

SEAMUS OFFERS WORDS
while the taste of codfish
lingers on his lips.

Another day, he says.
Another chance at life or death.
You and I are gamblers, Ann.
So what lies ahead do you suppose?

What lies ahead will be
a life more steadfast
than today,
but beyond these shores
I do not know,
though I find myself
wishing for the chance.

At that his hands tighten
over mine.
My breathing rises
before I look away.

Five days after the brig struck rock
the rock yields the last of its living.

Ten children died in wait for us.

Forty-eight children and women and men lost all told.

Sixty-four we carried to our house.

Ninety-nine we carried to the shore.

Despite what the merchant man would wish
we know the ways of numbers,
the price of their misfortune.

OUR HOUSE IS A BARREN REFUGE NOW,
filled with the sickly slumped together,
spilling out the doors.
Ashen, fragile,
silent but for raspy voices
wondering if all the food has gone.
What scraps remained were rationed
for the others left wanting on the beach.
Our Isle aux Morts has nothing more to give.

Tomorrow we'll fill the boats, says Father,
and row all we can to Port aux Basques.
For Father it's another day of doing
whatever must be done.

For what I must do I have no mind.
When dawn breaks Seamus rises
and beckons me away.
I follow him
as if I were the saved
and he the rescuer.

SEAMUS HAS THE FACE OF A WILD MAN
except his eyes,
more and more gentle
with each glance I take.
Along the shoreline rocks
just above the tidemark
there is comfort in the way he glances back

and in the way his hands wrap over mine
as if there were a pair of oars beneath them.

DON'T BE SKITTISH, ANN.
I'll not do anything to trouble you.

Then he kisses me, bold as brass.
There now, he says.

I am too stunned to answer him
but stare into his eager eyes
and purse my lips
because they tremble
in pleasure.

Must you stay in this place?
Do you not wish to see the world?

The world...
have I not dreamed such a dream

and have I not seen what becomes of those
who venture far from home?
Seamus, barely alive you were.
Look what has befallen you.

Seamus looks into my eyes.
Come away with me, Ann, he says
between his kisses.

WE'D MAKE A NEW WORLD.
In America, he says, and lets the
words fill my head —
Boston, New York, America.

I sit in the silence of the sun
as it rises over Isle aux Morts,
calm following the storm,
light glinting off the fairest sea
a world could ever claim.

I will teach you the ways of books, he says,
to recite the wisdom of the world,
to become a wonder to behold
in dresses more dazzling than the sun.

Then he smiles and holds my hand
and kisses me again.

WE ROW HAND OVER HAND
the nine miles to Port aux Basques.
He utters not a word.
His words are in the way his eyes
alight on mine
waiting for an answer.

The souls crowding us
collapse in silence.
Father bravely sings,
his voice stronger than
the day should ever warrant.

The sight of houses
prods them upright.
The thought of food
rouses unbelieving stares.
Father tells them —
these good people
will help us untangle your fate.

And thank God they do.
A dispatch is sent to a navy ship
farther up the coast

while we return to Isle aux Morts
for more silent boatloads of the famished.

THE ROWING IS ENDLESS.
The day is endless.
I collapse into sleep.

Come away with me, Ann,
he says again, huddled near me
when I awake.

But Seamus, what is the life we'll have?

What, indeed. Is that not the wonder of it?

But you have nothing to call your own.
Nothing but the clothes on your back
and a small lot of that.

He laughs.
No one has laughed for days.
It is the most wondrous sound
to ever touch my heart.

WHAT STIRS ME SO
what turns my lips
to return his smile
what beckons me away
to where no one
will know

his bruised
and battered body
cradles me
trusting me
to find
what stirs
within his heart

he kisses me
and rocks me
in the rhythm
of the sea

my eyes open
into this world
wishing him
to charm me
into another

his ways
lure me

unmoor me

OH, ANN, WHERE IS YOUR GOOD SENSE?
Mother says
when she sees
what has happened to my heart.

He hardly a man
and you but a young maid.

A young woman, says Father,
and a strong and fearless one at that.
To Ann's labor at the oars
these people owe their lives.

We cannot hold our girl forever, he says,
though he wipes a tear
as he turns away.

Out flows more of Mother's words —
it is so far that you might go
and never return,
and him poorer than the poor
and a Catholic at that.
Where is your good sense?

I WALK THE ROCKS ALONE
and face the sea alone
and sing the songs Father taught me.

My head turns in circles
and my heart
does not rest.
Will it ever?

You're not going, are you?
Tom it is, startling me
as much with his heartache
as his words.
You're needed here, he says.
Who will help us with the cod?

Who?
You are the man now, I tell him.
Your father's eldest son.

You're not the one for reading minds, he says.
You're the one for dreaming.

THE SONG I HEAR
is filled with doubt,
with an aching, heavy-hearted fear.

What of myself in days to come
without a talent to call my own?
What of myself without the sea,
unable to read or write of home?

The song I sing
is filled with pain,
with a haunting, wretched sting.

COME AWAY WITH ME, LOVER
stay with us, daughter
share my life, precious
share with us all

follow your heart, dreamer
take your part, sister
be true to yourself, Ann
but share with us all

His Majesty's ship Tyne
plying the coast
sails into Port aux Basques
embracing the Irish
with compassion
an ocean wide.
The Royal Navy
puts shoes on their feet
clothes on their backs
fills their empty bellies.

The *Tyne*'s pinnace and jolly boats
follow us to Isle aux Morts
to gather the last of the living.
Sent to pilot them past the jagged rocks
is Charles, son of our winter neighbor,
quietly sounding all the world like
a boy turned into a man.

Seamus lingers on the wharf
apart from the others
set to crowd aboard the *Tyne*,
set to sail for Halifax.
From there make passage to Quebec.
Their fearsome journey across the ocean
will find an end.
And they will see no more of Newfoundland.

ANN, COME AWAY.

Seamus, what am I to do?
Leave for a far-off world
perhaps worse than my own?

But Ann, your dreams —
do you not gaze out to sea
and yearn for what is beyond?

Seamus, you have nothing,
and I nothing
but the solid rock of home.

Ann, do you not love me?

I steer him away
from the crowds
that fill the wharf.

I know not, Seamus.
I know I love the way
your hands press mine
and your lips press mine,
the way my heart
fills my chest
at the sight of you.
Will it fill a lifetime?

He wraps me
in his arms
and lets our hearts fill,
and the overflow
seep into the ocean.

WHEN THE SHIP WEIGHS ANCHOR
I stand on shore
holding to the rock
of Newfoundland.

One hand of mine
that covered his
is in the air
waving, waving.
The other wipes
my eyes.

Father stands next to me.
Ann, he says, there'll be others.
You can be sure of that.

Perhaps there will,
though none so dauntless
and none so sweetly true.

Seamus fades into my horizon.

And I fade into his.

Historical Note

THE RESCUE by the Harvey family of 163 people ship-wrecked off Newfoundland's south coast in 1828 is a true story. To honor their heroism, a gold medal was struck by the Royal Humane Society in London.

George Harvey was quick to pass the medal over to his daughter, and to credit her with being the person most responsible for this amazing feat.

Ann is a true hero, though she has been little remembered, except for her name being given to a vessel of the Canadian Coast Guard, and except through the efforts of the people of Isle aux Morts, where today you can walk the Harvey Trail along the shoreline and gaze out at the treacherous reefs upon which the *Despatch* ran aground.

Ann and Seamus is in part a work of fiction. Little was recorded of the personal life of Ann Harvey or her family. We do know Ann married Charles Gillam, and that the couple eventually settled in Port aux Basques, where they raised a number of children. Ann died in 1860 at the age of forty-nine. Her grave is unmarked.

And we do know that ten years after the *Despatch* ordeal, another vessel, the *Rankin* out of Glasgow, Scotland, ran aground off Isle aux Morts. Again it was Ann Harvey and her father who faced a raging sea on a mission of rescue. Through their efforts all twenty-five passengers and crew were saved.

The story of Ann Harvey stands as a symbol of the steadfastness and bravery of the early settlers of Newfoundland and Labrador, who time and time again risked their own lives to save the lives of strangers.